THE LOST ONES

OTHER WORKS BY SAMUEL BECKETT
PUBLISHED BY GROVE PRESS

Cascando and Other Short Dramatic Pieces (Words and Music; Eh Joe; Play; Come and Go; Film [original version])

The Collected Works of Samuel Beckett

Endgame

Film, A Film Script

Happy Days

How It Is

Krapp's Last Tape and Other Dramatic Pieces (All That Fall; Embers [a play for radio]; Acts Without Words I and II [mimes])

Mallone Dies

Molloy

More Pricks Than Kicks

Murphy

Poems in English

Proust

Stories and Texts for Nothing

Three Novels (Molloy; Malone Dies; The Unnamable)

The Unnamable

Waiting for Godot

Watt

THE LOST ONES

Samuel Beckett

Translated from the original French by the author

GROVE PRESS, INC., NEW YORK

Originally published in French as *Le Depeupleur* by Les Editions
de Minuit, Paris, in 1971

First published in Great Britain in 1972 in the author's translation by
Calder & Boyars Ltd., London

ISBN: 0-394-17786-x

Library of Congress Catalog Card Number: 72-84341

First Evergreen Edition, 1972

First Printing

Printed and bound in the United States of America
by American Book–Stratford Press, New York

Distributed by Random House, Inc., New York

THE LOST ONES

A BODE where lost bodies roam each searching for its lost one. Vast enough for search to be in vain. Narrow enough for flight to be in vain. Inside a flattened cylinder fifty metres round and eighteen high for the sake of harmony. The light. Its dimness. Its yellowness. Its omnipresence as though every separate square centimetre were agleam of the some eighty thousand of total surface. Its restlessness at long intervals suddenly stilled like panting at the last. Then all go dead still. It is perhaps the end of their abode. A few seconds and all begins again. Consequences of this light for the searching eye. Consequences for the eye which having ceased to search is fastened to the ground or raised to the distant ceiling where none can be. The temperature. It oscillates with more measured beat between hot and cold. It passes from one extreme to the other in about four seconds. It too has its moments of stillness more or less hot or cold. They coincide with those of the light. Then all go dead still. It is perhaps the end of all. A few seconds and all begins again. Consequences of this climate for the skin. It shrivels. The bodies brush together with a rustle of dry leaves. The mucous membrane itself is affected. A kiss makes an indescribable sound. Those with stomach still to copulate strive in vain. But they will not give in. Floor and wall are of solid rubber or suchlike. Dash against them foot or fist or head and the sound is scarcely heard. Imagine then the silence of the steps. The only sounds worthy of the name result from the manipulation of the ladders or the thud of bodies striking against one another or of one against itself as when in sudden fury it beats its breast. Thus flesh and bone subsist. The ladders. These are the only objects. They are single without exception and vary greatly in size. The shortest measure not less than six metres. Some are fitted with a sliding extension. They are propped against the wall without regard to harmony. Bolt upright on the top rung of the tallest the tallest climbers can touch the ceiling with their fingertips. Its composition is no less familiar therefore than that of floor and wall. Dash a rung against it and the sound is scarcely heard. These ladders are in great demand.

9

At the foot of each at all times or nearly a little queue of climbers. And yet it takes courage to climb. For half the rungs are missing and this without regard to harmony. If only every second one were missing no great harm would be done. But the want of three in a row calls for acrobatics. These ladders are nevertheless in great demand and in no danger of being reduced to mere uprights runged at their extremities alone. For the need to climb is too widespread. To feel it no longer is a rare deliverance. The missing rungs are in the hands of a happy few who use them mainly for attack and self-defence. Their solitary attempts to brain themselves culminate at the best in brief losses of consciousness. The purpose of the ladders is to convey the searchers to the niches. Those whom these entice no longer climb simply to get clear of the ground. It is the custom not to climb two or more at a time. To the fugitive fortunate enough to find a ladder free it offers certain refuge until the clamours subside. The niches or alcoves. These are cavities sunk in that part of the wall which lies above an imaginary line running midway between floor and ceiling and features therefore of its upper half alone. A more or less wide mouth gives rapid access to a chamber of varying capacity but always sufficient for a body in reasonable command of its joints to enter in and similarly once in to crouch down after a fashion. They are disposed in irregular quincunxes roughly ten metres in diameter and cunningly out of line. Such harmony only he can relish whose long experience and detailed knowledge of the niches are

11

such as to permit a perfect mental image of the entire system. But it is doubtful that such a one exists. For each climber has a fondness for certain niches and refrains as far as possible from the others. A certain number are connected by tunnels opened in the thickness of the wall and attaining in some cases no fewer than fifty metres in length. But most have no other way out than the way in. It is as though at a certain stage discouragement had prevailed. To be noted in support of this wild surmise the existence of a long tunnel abandoned blind. Woe the body that rashly enters here to be compelled finally after long efforts to crawl back backwards as best it can the way it came. Not that this drama is peculiar to the unfinished tunnel. One has only to consider what inevitably must ensue when two bodies

12

enter a normal tunnel at the same time by opposite ends. Niches and tunnels are subject to the same light and climate as the rest of the abode. So much for a first aperçu of the abode.

*summary – casual/glance
detached – brief*

One body per square metre or two hundred bodies in all round numbers. Whether relatives near and far or friends in varying degree many in theory are acquainted. The gloom and press make recognition difficult. Seen from a certain angle these bodies are of four kinds. Firstly those perpetually in motion. Secondly those who sometimes pause. Thirdly those who short of being driven off never stir from the coign they have won and when driven off pounce on the first free one that offers and freeze again. That is not quite accurate. For if among these sedentary

13

the need to climb is dead it is
none the less subject to strange re-
surrections. The quidam then quits
his post in search of a free ladder or
to join the nearest or shortest queue.
The truth is that no searcher can
readily forego the ladder. Paradoxi-
cally the sedentary are those whose
acts of violence most disrupt the
cylinder's quiet. Fourthly those who
do not search or non-searchers sitting for the most part against the
wall in the attitude which wrung
from Dante one of his rare wan
smiles. By non-searchers and despite
the abyss to which this leads it is
finally impossible to understand
other than ex-searchers. To rid this _malignity_
notion of some of its virulence one
has only to suppose the need to
search no less resurrectable than
that of the ladder and those eyes to
all appearances for ever cast down or

14

closed possessed of the strange power suddenly to kindle again before passing face and body. But enough will always subsist to spell for this little people the extinction soon or late of its last remaining fires. A languishing happily unperceived because of its slowness and the resurgences that make up for it in part and the inattention of those concerned dazed by the passion preying on them still or by the state of languor into which imperceptibly they are already fallen. And far from being able to imagine their last state when every body will be still and every eye vacant they will come to it unwitting and be so unawares. Then light and climate will be changed in a way impossible to foretell. But the former may be imagined extinguished as purposeless and the latter fixed not far from freezing point. In cold darkness motionless flesh. So much roughly speaking for these bodies seen from a certain angle and for this notion and its consequences if it is maintained.

hardly

enough of this for a while as long as we ...

Inside a cylinder fifty metres round and eighteen high for the sake of harmony or a total surface of roughly twelve hundred square metres of which eight hundred mural. Not counting the niches and tunnels. Omnipresence of a dim yellow light shaken by a vertiginous tremolo between contiguous extremes. Temperature agitated by a like oscillation but thirty or forty times slower in virtue of which it falls rapidly from a maximum of twenty-five degrees approximately to a minimum of approximately five whence a regular variation of five degrees per second. That is not quite

16

accurate. For it is clear that at both extremes of the shuttle the difference can fall to as little as one degree only. But this remission never lasts more than a little less than a second. At great intervals suspension of the two vibrations fed no doubt from a single source and resumption together after a lull of varying duration but never exceeding ten seconds or thereabouts. Corresponding abeyance of all motion among the bodies in motion and heightened fixity of the motionless. Only objects fifteen single ladders propped against the wall at irregular intervals. In the upper half of the wall disposed quincuncially for the sake of harmony a score of niches some connected by tunnels.

From time immemorial rumour has it or better still the notion is abroad that there exists a way out. Those who no longer believe so are not immune from believing so again in accordance with the notion requiring as long as it holds that here all should die but with so gradual and to put it plainly so fluctuant a death as to escape the notice even of a visitor. Regarding the nature of this way out and its location two opinions divide without opposing all those still loyal to that old belief. One school swears by a secret passage branching from one of the tunnels and leading in the words of the poet to nature's sanctuaries. The other dreams of a trapdoor hidden in the hub of the ceiling giving access to a flue at the end of which the sun and other stars would still be shining. Conversion is frequent either way and such a one who at a given moment would hear of nothing but the tunnel may well a moment later hear of nothing but the trapdoor and a moment later still give himself the lie again. The fact remains none the less that of these two persuasions the former is declining in favour of the latter but in a manner so desultory and slow and of course with so little effect on the comportment of either sect that to perceive it one must be in the secret of the gods. This shift has logic on its side. For those who believe in a way out possible of access as via a tunnel it would be and even without any thought of putting it to account may be tempted by its quest. Whereas the partisans of the trapdoor are spared this demon by the fact that the hub of the ceiling is out of reach. Thus by insensible degrees the way out transfers from the tunnel to the ceiling prior to never having been. So much for a first aperçu of this credence so

19

singular in itself and by reason of the loyalty it inspires in the hearts of so many possessed. Its fatuous little light will be assuredly the last to leave them always assuming they are darkward bound.

Bolt upright on the top rung of the great ladder fully extended and reared against the wall the tallest climbers can touch the edge of the ceiling with their fingertips. On the same ladder planted perpendicular at the centre of the floor the same bodies would gain half a metre and so be enabled to explore at leisure the fabulous zone decreed out of reach and which therefore in theory is in no wise so. For such recourse to the ladder is conceivable. All that is needed is a score of determined volunteers joining forces to keep it upright with the help if necessary of other ladders acting as stay or struts. An instant of fraternity. But outside their explosions of violence this sentiment is as foreign to them as to butterflies. And this owing not so much to want of heart or intelligence as to the ideal preying on one and all. So much for this inviolable zenith where for amateurs of myth lies hidden a way out to earth and sky.

The use of the ladders is regulated by conventions of obscure origin which in their precision and the submission they exact from the climbers resemble laws. Certain infractions unleash against the culprit a collective fury surprising in creatures so peaceable on the whole and apart from the grand affair so careless of one another. Others on the contrary scarcely ruffle the general indifference. This at first sight is strange.

All rests on the rule against mounting the ladder more than one at a time. It remains taboo therefore to the climber waiting at its foot until such time as his predecessor has regained the ground. Idle to imagine the confusion that would result from the absence of such a rule or from its non-observance. But devised for the convenience of all there is no question of its applying without restriction or as a licence for the unprincipled climber to engross the ladder beyond what is reasonable. For without some form of curb he might take the fancy to settle down permanently in one of the niches or tunnels leaving behind him a ladder out of service for good and all. And were others to follow his example as inevitably they must the spectacle would finally be offered of one hundred and eighty-five searchers less the vanquished committed for all time to the ground. Not to mention the intolerable presence of properties serving no purpose. It is therefore understood that after a certain interval difficult to assess but unerringly timed by all the ladder is again available meaning at the disposal in the same conditions of him due next to climb easily recognizable by his position at the head of the queue and so much the worst for the abuser. The situation of this latter having lost his ladder is delicate indeed and seems to exclude a priori his ever returning to the ground. Happily sooner or later he succeeds in doing so thanks to a further provision giving priority at all times to descent over ascent. He has therefore merely to watch at the mouth of his niche for a ladder to present itself and immediately start down quite easy in his mind knowing full well that whoever below is on the point of mounting if not already on his way up will give way in his favour. The worst that can befall him is a long vigil because of the ladders' mobility. It is indeed rare for a climber when it comes to his turn to content himself with the same niche as his predecessor and this for obvious reasons that will appear in due course. But rather he makes off with his ladder followed by the queue and plants it under one or other of the five niches available by reason of the difference in number between these and the ladders. But to return to the unfortunate having outstayed his time it is clear that his chances of rapid redescent will be increased though far from doubled if thanks to a tunnel he disposes of two niches from which to watch. Though even in this event he usually prefers and invariably if the tunnel is a long one to plump for one only lest a ladder should present itself at one or the other and he still crawling between the two. But the ladders do not serve only as vehicles to the niches and tunnels and those whom these have ceased if only temporarily to entice use them simply to get clear of the ground. They mount to the level of their choice and there stay and settle standing as a rule with their faces to the wall. This family of climbers too is liable to exceed the allotted time. It is in order then for him due next for the ladder to climb in the wake of the offender and by means of one or more thumps on the back bring him back to a sense of his surroundings. Upon which he unfailingly hastens to descend preceded by his successor who has then merely to take over the ladder subject to the usual conditions. This docility in the abuser shows clearly that the abuse is not deliberate but due to a temporary derangement of his inner timepiece easy to understand and therefore to forgive. Here is the reason why this in reality infrequent infringement whether on the part of those who push on up to the niches and tunnels or of those who halt on the way never gives rise to the fury vented on the wretch with no better sense than to climb before his time and yet whose precipitancy one would have thought quite as understandable and consequently forgivable as the converse excess. This is indeed strange. But what is at stake is the fundamental principle forbidding ascent more than one at a time the repeated violation of which would soon transform the abode into a pandemonium.

Whereas the belated return to the ground hurts finally none but the laggard himself. So much for a first aperçu of the climbers' code.

Similarly the transport of the ladders is not left to the good pleasure of the carriers who are required to hug the wall at all times eddywise. This is a rule no less strict than the prohibition to climb more than one at a time and not lightly to be broken. Nothing more natural. For if for the sake of the shortcut it were permitted to carry the ladder slap through the press or skirting the wall at will in either direction life in the cylinder would soon become untenable. All along the wall therefore a belt about one metre wide is reserved for the carriers. To this zone those also are confined who wait their turn to climb and must close their ranks and flatten themselves as best they can with their backs to the wall so as not to encroach on the arena proper.

It is curious to note the presence within this belt of a certain number of sedentary searchers sitting or standing against the wall. Dead to the ladders to all intents and purposes and a source of annoyance for both climbers and carriers they are nevertheless tolerated. The fact is that these sort of semi-sages among whom all ages are to be admired from old age to infancy inspire in those still fitfully fevering if not a cult at least a certain deference. They cling to this as to a homage due to them and are morbidly susceptible to the least want of consideration. A sedentary searcher stepped on instead of over is capable of such an outburst of fury as to throw the entire cylinder into a ferment. Cleave also to the wall both sitting and standing four vanquished out of five. They may be walked on without their reacting.

To be noted finally the care taken by the searchers in the arena not to overflow on the climbers' territory. When weary of searching among the throng they turn towards this zone it is only to skirt with measured tread its imaginary edge devouring with their eyes its occupants. Their slow round counter-carrierwise creates a second even narrower belt respected in its turn by the main body of searchers. Which suitably lit from above would give the impression at times of two narrow rings turning in opposite directions about the teeming precinct.

One body per square metre of available surface or two hundred bodies in all round numbers. Bodies of either sex and all ages from old age to infancy. Sucklings who having no longer to suck huddle at gaze in the lap or sprawled on the ground in precocious postures. Others a little more advanced crawl searching among the legs. Picturesque detail a woman with white hair still young to judge by her thighs leaning against the wall with eyes closed in abandonment and mechanically clasping to her breast a mite who strains away in an effort to turn its head and look behind. But such tiny ones are comparatively few. None looks within himself where none can be. Eyes cast down or closed signify abandonment and are confined to the vanquished. These precisely to be counted on the fingers of one hand

30

are not necessarily still. They may stray unseeing through the throng indistinguishable to the eye of flesh from the still unrelenting. These recognize them and make way. They may wait their turn at the foot of the ladders and when it comes ascend to the niches or simply leave the ground. They may crawl blindly in the tunnels in search of nothing. But normally abandonment freezes them both in space and in their pose whether standing or sitting as a rule profoundly bowed. It is this makes it possible to tell them from the sedentary devouring with their eyes in heads dead still each body as it passes by. Standing or sitting they cleave to the wall all but one in the arena stricken rigid in the midst of the fevering. These recognize him and keep their distance. The spent eyes may have fits of the old craving just as those who having renounced the ladder suddenly take to it again. So true it is that when in the cylinder what little is possible is not so it is merely no longer so and in the least less the all of nothing if this notion is maintained. Then the eyes suddenly start to search afresh as famished as the unthinkable first day until for no clear reason they as suddenly close again or the head falls. Even so a great heap of sand sheltered from the wind lessened by three grains every second year and every following increased by two if this notion is maintained. If then the vanquished have still some way to go what can be said of the others and what better name be given them than the fair name of searchers? Some and indeed by far the greater number never pause except when they line up for a ladder or watch out at the mouth of a niche. Some come to rest from time to time all but the unceasing eyes. As for the sedentary if they never stir from the coign they have won it is because they have calculated their best chance is there and if they seldom or never ascend to the niches and tunnels it is because they have done so too often in vain or come there too often to grief. An intelligence would be tempted to see in these the next vanquished and continuing in its stride to require of those still perpetually in motion that they all soon or late one after another be as those who sometimes pause and of these that they finally be as the sedentary and of the sedentary that they be in the end as the vanquished and of the two hundred vanquished thus obtained that all in due course each in his turn be well and truly vanquished for good and all each frozen in his place and attitude. But let these families be numbered in order of maturity and experience shows that it is possible to graduate from one to three skipping two and from one to four skipping two or three or both and from two to four skipping three. In the other direction the ill-vanquished may at long intervals and with each relapse more briefly revert to the state of the sedentary who in their turn count a few chronic waverers prone to succumb to the ladder again while remaining dead to the arena. But never again will they ceaselessly come and go who now at long intervals come to rest without ceasing to search with their eyes. In the beginning then unthinkable as the end all roamed without respite including the nurselings in so far as they were borne except of course those already

at the foot of the ladders or frozen in
the tunnels the better to listen or
crouching all eyes in the niches and
so roamed a vast space of time
impossible to measure until a first
came to a standstill followed by a
second and so on. But as to at this
moment of time and there will be no
other numbering the faithful who
endlessly come and go impatient of
the least repose and those who every
now and then stand still and the
sedentary and the so-called vanquished may it suffice to state that at
this moment of time to the nearest
body in spite of the press and gloom
the first are twice as many as the
second who are three times as many
as the third who are four times as
many as the fourth namely five vanquished in all. Relatives and friends
are well represented not to speak
of mere acquaintances. Press and

gloom make recognition difficult. Man and wife are strangers two paces apart to mention only this most intimate of all bonds. Let them move on till they are close enough to touch and then without pausing on their way exchange a look. If they recognize each other it does not appear. Whatever it is they are searching for it is not that.

What first impresses in this gloom is the sensation of yellow it imparts not to say of sulphur in view of the associations. Then how it throbs with constant unchanging beat and fast but not so fast that the pulse is no longer felt. And finally much later that ever and anon there comes a momentary lull. The effect of those brief and rare respites is unspeakably dramatic to put it mildly. Those who never know a moment's rest

36

stand rooted to the spot often in extravagant postures and the stillness heightened tenfold of the sedentary and vanquished makes that which is normally theirs seem risible in comparison. The fists on their way to smite in anger or discouragement freeze in their arcs until the scare is past and the blow can be completed or volley of blows. Similarly without entering into tedious details those surprised in the act of climbing or carrying a ladder or making unmakable love or crouched in the niches or crawling in the tunnels as the case may be. But a brief ten seconds at most and the throbbing is resumed and all is as before. Those interrupted in their coming and going start coming and going again and the motionless relax. The lovers buckle to anew and the fists carry on where they left off. The murmur cut off as though by a switch fills the cylinder again. Among all the components the sum of which it is the ear finally distinguishes a faint stridulence as of insects which is that of the light itself and the one invariable. Between the extremes that delimit the vibration the difference is of two or three candles at the most. So that the sensation of yellow is faintly tinged with one of red. Light in a word that not only dims but blurs into the bargain. It might safely be maintained that the eye grows used to these conditions and in the end adapts to them were it not that just the contrary is to be observed in the slow deterioration of vision ruined by this fiery flickering murk and by the incessant straining for ever vain with concomitant moral distress and its repercussion on the organ. And were it possible to

38

follow over a long enough period of
time eyes blue for preference as being
the most perishable they would be
seen to redden more and more in an
ever widening glare and their pupils
little by little to dilate till the whole
orb was devoured. And all by such
slow and insensible degrees to be
sure as to pass unperceived even by
those most concerned if this notion
is maintained. And the thinking
being coldly intent on all these data
and evidences could scarcely escape
at the close of his analysis the mis-
taken conclusion that instead of
speaking of the vanquished with the
slight taint of pathos attaching to
the term it would be more correct to
speak of the blind and leave it at
that. Once the first shocks of sur-
prise are finally past this light is
further unusual in that far from
evincing one or more visible or

39

hidden sources it appears to emanate from all sides and to permeate the entire space as though this were uniformly luminous down to its least particle of ambient air. To the point that the ladders themselves seem rather to shed than to receive light with this slight reserve that light is not the word. No other shadows then than those cast by the bodies pressing on one another wilfully or from necessity as when for example on a breast to prevent its being lit or on some private part the hand descends with vanished palm. Whereas the skin of a climber alone on his ladder or in the depths of a tunnel glistens all over with the same red-yellow glister and even some of its folds and recesses in so far as the air enters in. With regard to the temperature its oscillation is between much wider extremes and at a much lower fre-

40

quency since it takes not less than four seconds to pass from its minimum of five degrees to its maximum of twenty-five and inversely namely an average of only five degrees per second. Does this mean that with every passing second there is a rise or fall of five degrees exactly neither more nor less? Not quite. For it is clear there are two periods in the scale namely from twenty-one degrees on on the way up and from nine on on the way down when this difference will not be reached. Out of the eight seconds therefore required for a single rise and fall it is only during a bare six and a half that the bodies suffer the maximum increment of heat or cold which with the help of a little addition or better still division works out nevertheless at some twenty years respite per century in this domain. There is

41

something disturbing at first sight in the relative slowness of this vibration compared to that of the light. But this is a disturbance analysis makes short work of. For on due reflection the difference to be considered is not one of speed but of space travelled. And if that required of the temperature were reduced to the equivalent of a few candles there would be nothing to choose mutatis mutandis between the two effects. But that would not answer the needs of the cylinder. So all is for the best. The more so as the two storms have this in common that when one is cut off as though by magic then in the same breath the other also as though again the two were connected somewhere to a single commutator. For in the cylinder alone are certitudes to be found and without nothing but mystery. At vast intervals then the bodies enjoy ten seconds at most of unbroken warmth or cold or between the two. But this cannot be truly accounted for respite so great is the other tension then.

The bed of the cylinder comprises three distinct zones separated by clear-cut mental or imaginary frontiers invisible to the eye of flesh. First an outer belt roughly one metre wide reserved for the climbers and strange to say favoured by most of the sedentary and vanquished. Next a slightly narrower inner belt where those weary of searching in mid-cylinder slowly revolve in Indian file intent on the periphery. Finally the arena proper representing an area of one hundred and fifty square metres round numbers and chosen hunting ground of the majority. Let numbers be assigned to these three zones and it appears clearly that from the third to the second and inversely the searcher moves at will whereas on entering and leaving the first he is held to a certain discipline. One example among a thousand of the harmony that reigns in the cylinder between order and licence. Thus access to the climbers' reserve is authorized only when one of them leaves it to rejoin the searchers of the arena or exceptionally those of the intermediate zone. While infringement of this rule is rare it does none the less occur as when for example a particularly nervous searcher can no longer resist the lure of the niches and tries to steal in among the climbers without the warrant of a departure. Whereupon he is unfailingly ejected by the queue nearest to the point of trespass and the matter goes no further. No

44

choice then for the searcher wishing to join the climbers but to watch for his opportunity among the searchers of the intermediate zone or searcher-watchers or simply watchers. So much for access to the ladders. In the other direction the passage is not free either and once among the climbers the watcher is there for some time and more precisely the highly variable time it takes to advance from the tail to the head of the queue adopted. For no less than the freedom for each body to climb is the obligation once in the queue of its choice to queue on to the end. Any attempt to leave prematurely is sharply countered by the other members and the offender put back in his place. But once at the very foot of the ladder with between him and it only one more return to the ground the aspirant is free to rejoin the

45

searchers of the arena or exceptionally the watchers of the intermediate zone without opposition. It is therefore on those at the head of their lines as being the most likely to create the vacancy so ardently desired that the eyes of the second-zone watchers are fixed as they burn to enter the first. The objects of this scrutiny continue so up to the moment they exercise their right to the ladder and take it over. For the climber may reach the head of the queue with the firm resolve to ascend and then feel this melt little by little and gather in its stead the urge to depart but still without the power to decide him till the very last moment when his predecessor is actually on the way down and the ladder virtually his at last. To be noted also the possibility for the climber to leave the queue once he has reached

46

the head and yet not leave the zone. This merely requires his joining one of the other fourteen queues at his disposal or more simply still his returning to the tail of his own. But it is exceptional for a body in the first place to leave its queue and in the second having exceptionally done so not to leave the zone. No alternative then once among the climbers but to stay there at least the time it takes to advance from the the last place to the first of the chosen queue. This time varies according to the length of the latter and the more or less prolonged occupation of the ladder. Some users keep it till the last moment. For others one half or any other fraction of this time is enough. The short queue is not necessarily the most rapid and such a one starting fifth may well find himself first before such another starting tenth assuming of course they start together. This being so no wonder that the choice of the queue is determined by considerations having nothing to do with its length. Not that all choose nor even the greater number. The tendency would be rather to join straightway the queue nearest to the point of penetration on condition however that this does not involve motion against the stream. For one entering this zone head-on the nearest queue is on the right and if it does not please it is only by going right that a more pleasing can be found. Some could thus revolve through thousands of degrees before settling down to wait were it not for the rule forbidding them to exceed a single circuit. Any attempt to elude it is quelled by the queue nearest to the point of full circle and the culprit

48

compelled to join its ranks since
obviously the right to turn back is
denied him too. That a full round
should be authorized is eloquent of
the tolerant spirit which in the
cylinder tempers discipline. But
whether chosen or first to hand the
queue must be suffered to the end
before the climber may leave the
zone. First chance of departure
therefore at any moment between
arrival at head of queue and predecessor's return to ground. There
remains to clarify in this same con-
text the situation of the body which
having accomplished its queue and
let pass the first chance of departure
and exercised its right to the ladder
returns to the ground. It is now free
again to depart without further ado
but with no compulsion to do so. And
to remain among the climbers it has
merely to join again in the same

49

conditions as before the queue so lately left with departure again possible from the moment the head is reached. And should it for some reason or another feel like a little change of queue and ladder it is entitled for the purpose of fixing its choice to a further full circuit in the same way as on first arrival and in the same conditions with this slight difference that having already suffered one queue to the end it is free at any moment of the new revolution to leave the zone. And so on infinitely. Whence theoretically the possibility for those already among the climbers never to leave and never to arrive for those not yet. That there exists no regulation tending to forestall such injustice shows clearly it can never be more than temporary. As indeed it cannot. For the passion to search is such that no place may be left unsearched. To the watcher nevertheless on the qui vive for a departure the wait may seem interminable. Sometimes unable to endure it any longer and fortified by the long vacation he renounces the ladder and resumes his search in the arena. So much roughly speaking for the main ground divisions and the duties and prerogatives of the bodies in their passage from one to another. All has not been told and never shall be. What principle of priority obtains among the watchers always in force and eager to profit by the first departure from among the climbers and whose order of arrival on the scene cannot be established by the queue impracticable in their case or by any other means? Is there not reason to fear a saturation of the intermediate zone and what would be its consequences for the bodies as a whole and particularly for those of the arena thus cut off from the ladders? Is not the cylinder doomed in a more or less distant future to a state of anarchy given over to fury and violence? To these questions and many more the answers are clear and easy to give. It only remains to dare. The sedentary call for no special remark since only the ladders can wean them from their fixity. The vanquished are obviously in no way concerned.

The effect of this climate on the soul is not to be underestimated. But it suffers certainly less than the skin whose entire defensive system from sweat to goose bumps is under constant stress. It continues none the less feebly to resist and indeed honourably compared to the eye which with the best will in the world it is difficult not to consign at the close of all its efforts to nothing short of blindness. For skin in its own way as it is not to mention its humours and lids it has not merely one adversary to contend with. This desiccation of the envelope robs nudity of much of its charm as pink turns grey and transforms into a rustling of nettles the natural succulence of flesh against flesh. The mucous membrane itself is affected which would not greatly matter were it not for its hampering effect on the work of love. But even from this point of view no great harm is done so rare is erection in the cylinder. It does occur none the less followed by more or less happy penetration in the nearest tube. Even man and wife may sometimes be seen in virtue of the law of probabilities to come together again in this way without their knowledge. The spectacle then is one to be remembered of frenzies prolonged in pain and hopelessness long beyond what even the most gifted lovers can achieve in camera. For male or female all are acutely aware how rare the occasion is and how unlikely to recur. But here too the desisting and deathly still in attitudes verging at times on the obscene whenever the vibrations cease and for as long as this crisis lasts. Stranger still at such times all the questing eyes that suddenly go still and fix their stare on the void or on some old abomination as for instance other eyes and then the long looks exchanged by those fain to look away. Irregular intervals of such length separate these lulls that for forgetters the likes of these each is the first. Whence invariably the same vivacity of reaction as to the

54

end of a world and the same brief amaze when the twofold storm resumes and they start to search again neither glad nor even sorry.

Seen from below the wall presents an unbroken surface all the way round and up to the ceiling. And yet its upper half is riddled with niches. This paradox is explained by the levelling effect of the dim omnipresent light. None has even been known to seek out a niche from below. The eyes are seldom raised and when they are it is to the ceiling. Floor and ceiling bear no sign or mark apt to serve as a guide. The feet of the ladders pitched always at the same points leave no trace. The same is true of the skulls and fists dashed against the wall. Even did such marks exist the light would prevent their being seen. The climber

making off with his ladder to plant it
elsewhere relies largely on feel. He is
seldom out by more than a few centi-
metres and never by more than a
metre at most because of the way the
niches are disposed. On the spur of
his passion his agility is such that
even this deviation does not prevent
him from gaining the nearest if not
the desired niche and thence though
with greater labour from regaining
the ladder for the descent. There
does none the less exist a north in the
guise of one of the vanquished or
better one of the women vanquished
or better still the woman vanquished.
She squats against the wall with her
head between her knees and her legs
in her arms. The left hand clasps the
right shinbone and the right the left
forearm. The red hair tarnished by
the light hangs to the ground. It
hides the face and whole front of the

body down to the crutch. The left foot is crossed on the right. She is the north. She rather than some other among the vanquished because of her greater fixity. To one bent for once on taking his bearings she may be of help. For the climber averse to avoidable acrobatics a given niche may lie so many paces or metres to east or west of the woman vanquished without of course his naming her thus or otherwise even in his thoughts. It goes without saying that only the vanquished hide their faces though not all without exception. Standing or sitting with head erect some content themselves with opening their eyes no more. It is of course forbidden to withhold the face or other part from the searcher who demands it and may without fear of resistance remove the hand from the flesh it hides or raise the lid to

57

examine the eye. Some searchers there are who join the climbers with no thought of climbing and simply in order to inspect at close hand one or more among the vanquished or sedentary. The hair of the woman vanquished has thus many a time been gathered up and drawn back and the head raised and the face laid bare and whole front of the body down to the crutch. The inspection once completed it is usual to put everything carefully back in place as far as possible. It is enjoined by a certain ethics not to do unto others what coming from them might give offence. This precept is largely observed in the cylinder in so far as it does not jeopardize the quest which would clearly be a mockery if in case of doubt it were not possible to check certain details. Direct action with a view to their elucidation is generally reserved for the persons of the sedentary and vanquished. Face or back to the wall these normally offer but a single aspect and so may have to be turned the other way. But wherever there is motion as in the arena or among the watchers and the possibility of encompassing the object there is no call for such manipulations. There are times of course when a body has to be brought to a stand and disposed in a certain position to permit the inspection at close hand of a particular part or the search for a scar or birthblot for example. To be noted finally the immunity in this respect of those queueing for a ladder. Obliged for want of space to huddle together over long periods they appear to the observer a mere jumble of mingled flesh. Woe the rash searcher who carried away by his passion dare lay a finger on the least among them. Like a single body the whole queue falls on the offender. Of all the scenes of violence the cylinder has to offer none approaches this.

So on infinitely until towards the unthinkable end if this notion is maintained a last body of all by feeble fits and starts is searching still. There is nothing at first sight to distinguish him from the others dead still where they stand or sit in abandonment beyond recall. Lying down is unheard of in the cylinder and this pose solace of the vanquished is for ever denied them here. Such privation is partly to be explained by the dearth of floor space namely a little under one square metre at the disposal of each body and not to be eked out by that of the niches and tunnels reserved for the search alone. Thus the prostration of those withered ones filled with the horror of contact and compelled to brush together without ceasing is denied its natural end. But the persistence of the twofold vibration suggests that in this old abode all is not yet quite for the best. And sure enough there he stirs this last of all if a man and slowly draws himself up and some time later opens his burnt eyes. At the foot of the ladders propped against the wall with scant regard to harmony no climber waits his turn. The aged vanquished of the third zone has none about him now but others in his image motionless and bowed. The mite still in the white-haired woman's clasp is no more than a shadow in her lap. Seen from the front the red head sunk to the uttermost exposes part of the nape. There he opens then his eyes this last of all if a man and some time later threads his way to that first among the vanquished so often taken for a guide. On his knees he parts the heavy hair and raises the unresisting head. Once devoured the face thus laid bare the eyes at a touch of the thumbs open without demur. In those calm wastes he lets his wander till they are the first to close and the head relinquished falls back into its place. He himself after a pause impossible to time finds at last his place and pose whereupon dark descends and at the same instant the temperature comes to rest not far from freezing point. Hushed in the same breath the faint stridulence mentioned above whence suddenly such silence as to drown all the faint breathings put together. So much roughly speaking for the last state of the cylinder and of this little people of searchers one first of whom if a man in some unthinkable past for the first time bowed his head if this notion is maintained.

Beckett —

Near Dublin

1906   - Fox Rock ↑ 13th April Good Friday

Middle class protestant

Trinity College
Campbell College in Belfast — 1st teaching
Beckett became Joyce's secretary
Friends + mutual friends
Horoscope — 1930 1st published work
Les Kids - 1st drama script
More Pricks than kicks —
Murphy — 1st Novel 1930

1946-1950 — trilogy + Waiting for Godot

1952 — Waiting for Godot published in Paris

1953 — opened

54 — Godot - New York Published

57 — Endgame

58 — Kropps Last Tape

69 = Received Nobel Prize for Lit.

. Lost ones = First published work after Nobel Prize